TALES OF A HOTELWALLAH

SANDIP MUKHERJEE

Copyright © Sandip Mukherjee 2021
All Rights Reserved.

ISBN 9781684943647

This book has been published with all efforts taken to make the material error-free after the consent of the author. However, the author and the publisher do not assume and hereby disclaim any liability to any party for any loss, damage, or disruption caused by errors or omissions, whether such errors or omissions result from negligence, accident, or any other cause.

While every effort has been made to avoid any mistake or omission, this publication is being sold on the condition and understanding that neither the author nor the publishers or printers would be liable in any manner to any person by reason of any mistake or omission in this publication or for any action taken or omitted to be taken or advice rendered or accepted on the basis of this work. For any defect in printing or binding the publishers will be liable only to replace the defective copy by another copy of this work then available.

*To **all colleagues in hospitality*** *who daily dream to see that delight on faces of guests they serve*

Contents

Foreword for a Friend — 7
Preface — 13

1. The Sting — 18
2. Brand Custodians — 28
3. The Case of the Missing Guest — 41
4. Black Dog — 54
5. Found and Lost — 63
6. Close Encounter — 69
7. Just Another Day — 78
8. Accounts Receivable — 86
9. The Practical Nun — 97
10. Cyber Crime — 106

Foreword for a Friend

No. This isn't a foreword for a book. I am writing this for a friend; actually, two lovely friends that me and my wife Susmita got to know over years. We have both been itinerant people. If you did a worldwide poll for how many hotel room nights were ours, that would put us in the top quadrant for sure. Having become empty nesters at a relatively early age, and Susmita being a writer who could take her work wherever, I always coaxed her into joining me on most of my work-related tours. That is how we got to know Sandip when he was the man running the Taj Blue Diamond in Pune. It was a small hotel and we often stayed there. Because it was small, it packed more of the Taj goodness in a small space. However infrequent a guest, there was no missing the ever-affable Sandip Mukherjee, General Manager, as you went in and out, somewhere in the lobby, the coffee shop, or the Chinese restaurant, waiting to say hello. Hoteliers are trained to be nice. But Sandip was different. The man had a genuine liking for strangers, he was also authentic in a way that made me pause.

Each time I returned to the Blue Diamond, I looked for him. Susmita too became fond of him. He had eclectic reading taste, we liked that. He and his wife Kalpana had two young girls and we loved that, having two of those ourselves. Then one day, Sandip went away from the Blue Diamond. But unlike the many events in life, of *knowing someone* and eventually *fading out of it*, we remained in touch with him. From Pune, he went to the Taj Langkawi in Malaysia. Every so often, he would say, come and stay with us. Every time, we said *yes, yes* but it was the kind of *yes, yes,* you say politely. That changed one day when Susmita's mother was convalescing after her cancer treatment. She was a beautiful woman who was the editor of a very successful magazine. She was very fond of traveling her entire life. She and my father-in-law had trotted the world on frugal savings squirreled away. Growing up, Susmita sometimes heard her mother say how much she would like to have that one overseas holiday without having to worry about running out of money. Even as that didn't happen while she was active, we now decided to give her a lovely holiday to remember. We called Sandip, and took him into confidence for getting the little extra care that we knew we would get anyway. But what awaited us on our arrival wasn't what we had ever expected.

Sandip and Kalpana were there at the jetty from where we would take the boat to the island resort. Seeing Susmita's parents, they shone like they were meeting their own. Kalpana, took Ma's hand in her own, signalling that from now, she was in her care. Tired from an overnight flight, Ma fumbled for a moment, trying to get into the boat. Kalpana asked her to remove her sandals and simply held them in her other hand as she and Sandip helped her in. From then on, until we left the resort, she was their mother, not ours. It was the first time we were meeting Kalpana, and we were overwhelmed. The many small things Sandip and Kalpana had thought through for her, keeping her in the centre of everything, without it being evident or obtrusive, told us volumes about the two beautiful people who were not hoteliers, they were friends, great human beings we were deeply honoured to have in our lives.

The stay at Langkawi was idyllic. We paced ourselves through the soft drift of time through Ma's frail fingers.

Sandip and Kalpana spoke to her, listened to her, took the parents for a visit to the butterfly park, showed them the hornbills – "Aunty, they pair for life", arranged a dinner by the beach where Sandip had set up his personal telescope through which, between the white wine and the red, Ma was shown the craters on the Moon.

She was gently floating. It was one of the nicest trips for her, made memorable by two people who had never seen her before.

While we were on the island, I spent time observing the Mukherjee couple very closely. All my life, I have been curious about people in the service industry who are required to smile, to be attentive, to please, to pamper because they are paid to so. But even as they are so-called professionals, they are human beings. Behind the smile, sometimes there is a tear somewhere left behind.

Behind the desire to deliver at the drop of a whim of the guest, in their own lives, there are many packages often returned, with the "sender gone long back with no forwarding address". Through it all, there are a few who do what they do, not as their job but as their calling. And come to think of it, Kalpana, though she had worked in the hospitality industry during her professional career, wasn't even a Taj employee on that island. But she was the mother to every staff member, she was their joy and one had to be observant to know that she was getting the affective regard, not as the General Manager's wife but as someone who deeply cared for every staff member, from the buggy man and the janitor, the gardener, and the boatman.

After that memorable trip, Ma started fading and no longer were we talking about the one vacation in which she needn't have to think of a budget. But Sandip and Kalpana always stayed with her in her gentle memory.

In Langkawi, his assignment kept getting extended, past his official retirement age. Finally they came back, he retired, They were to go to Aurangabad, he wanted to teach there, she wanted to do all the things she could never do in all those years and of course came along the great joys bundled as grandkids. One day, we learnt, they have moved to an apartment in Kolkata. Susmita and I went to see them. We had a joyous little tea party. And Sandip was excited to see us because he had to talk to us about this book of his which was finally coming together, his inn-keeper's diary. Of the many beautiful, some anxious, some hilarious recollections of an entire life spent looking after real people, fake people, rich people, ordinary people. Seeing the world through them, seeing the world with them. Not for a moment judgmental, not compromising on their need for anonymity. Making another world come alive from under a veneer, a world that is there everywhere in the hotel but one that is invisible to us even as we may spend a night, breeze in and out for a drink, settle down to the table by the window to do a deal over dinner.

Sandip (and Kalpana)'s sensitively woven book will check you in and keep you charmed. You will be enchanted with the many facets of a world into which we pour in so many of our nights and in its dawn, there is always a new dawn, made possible with the attending orchestra of the front office, the housekeeping, the room service, the restaurant, the banquet, the doorman and everyone else who make you believe, *you* are the centre of their Universe.

The check-out time for this book in your hands is 12 noon, but Sandip will give you a late check out if you need.

So read on. No hurry.

Subroto Bagchi
Bhubaneswar,
India
November 1, 2021

Preface

In four decades and more of exciting travels and travails, hosting friendly guests and fusspots, managing successful events and failures, latching on to secrets of casual and regular guests, a specific thought always crossed my mind.

One day I must share some of these fascinating incidents with others.

Not all, as that would be inappropriate, but some that would at least unravel a bit of what a hotelwallah indeed comes across in his daily walk of life.

Early on in our career when we started the journey of inn-keeping there was not much acknowledgement of our vocation, possibly as tourism was still regarded an insignificant contributor towards national development.

Much has changed since then. Resorts and hotels of all hues have sprung up, international players have set up shop and some of our own national brands are accepted as centres of service excellence thus claiming their rightful position in the world of tourism. Finally tourism has got its due with at least one state declaring it as an industry.

Despite this, to many prolific consumers of the various products of hospitality, what exactly constitutes a day in the life of such professionals who meet, greet and serve them, remain a mystery.

Not many realise that in a single day's work hospitality teams serve state heads, celebrities, academics, corporates, socially responsible citizens among others. However, at the same breath they strive hard to satisfy the sinister, litigant, troublesome, insinuating – in brief some of the most difficult sort as well!

C'est la vie…

The collection of these incidents are real life snippets and are largely centered around resorts and hotels that I have been fortunate to serve while few are contributions from my colleagues who were kind enough to share them with me.

Names and locations of course have been *masked* for privacy.

I must thank Rajen my good friend and colleague from Malaysia, Ashok Sood from Mumbai, Pravash, Naba and Chandan – all from our alma mater, the Institute of Hotel Management in Kolkata.

Chandan in particular has painstakingly spent hour upon hour correcting the script and putting these memories together, in a reader friendly format.

A huge appreciation is due to the young team at *Notion* my publishers for letting this venture see the light of the day.

My wife Kalpana, daughters Nupur and Madhavi, and their husbands Rohit and Subhash all deserve a round of thanks for their ever loving support.

Above all the biggest round of thanks indeed goes to Mr. and Mrs. Subroto Bagchi, founder of the fabulous tech enterprise - Mindtree Consulting and a favourite author of mine.

Mrs. Bagchi in her own right is an award winning author of tremendous standing herself.

Both have always been very important and dearly loved guests of ours at various properties that we were based out of.

During one of their holidays with us, the entire family including his in laws, encouraged me to keep a record of and publish some interesting facets of our business. They asked me to pen down unusual, funny and insightful incidents that we in hotels and resorts encounter time to time.

This is truly a tribute to them, having egged me to come out with a bunch of experiences and hopefully this shall not be the last.

I will be happy to know if the stories put a momentary smile on your lips and gave an insight into lengths to which hospitality colleagues can stretch for guests' delight.

This indeed is what makes them so special.

Happy reading, I eagerly await your comments.

Sandip Mukherjee
New Town, Kolkata,
India
November 1, 2021
copavillaglobal@gmail.com

"I'm going to make him an offer he can't refuse."

The Godfather, 1972

The Sting

Why am I alone here? Thought Raj to himself.

Dressed in smart black tuxedo and a frilled shirt with a deep maroon silk bow Raj was waiting for others to join him at Roxanne's, the hottest night spot in town. His GM had asked him to grace the occasion by being the Chief Judge for Miss China Penang and he was mighty pleased that of all his colleagues his boss singularly gave him that honour.

Raj was the Banquets Head for a five-star popular hotel in the hottest area in town – Batu Ferringhi, and his newly posted dashing European GM and he got along famously.

He was to get married in a few weeks' time and during those days he was on a spree of organising the occassion and personally distributing invites for the event of his life.

"Do me a favour Raj," said Helmut when Raj went to hand over his marriage invite to him.

"I was to be the Chief Judge this weekend at Roxanne's for their Miss China show. Please replace me, I need to take Julianna out for a quiet dinner and just did not have the time this past one month."

With this he handed over a smart leather folder which had details of this famous night club and an invite to the show. "I will handle the changeover of names," Helmut said. "Just leave that to me. Go over the documents and that describes the sequence of the functions. It has CVs of the contestants and what you need to do that night."

Raj was elated, he had never been to Roxanne's and though he knew this was *the* night spot in town he could not believe he would be the star of the show!

"Thank you Helmut, this is wonderful," said Raj.

"Very well then, thanks for inviting me over to your marriage, see you around", said Helmut and they parted happily.

A day later as promised, Raj received a black and gold bordered envelope with an invite which had his name in bold stating he was now the Chief Judge for this prestigious event.

Raj was jubilant!

A couple of days later he received a parking sticker, instructions to reach the club, a Judge's badge and a few other trivia related to the event. A thank you letter with complimentary restaurant and bar vouchers of happening spots in Penang followed the very next day from the organisers.

Raj was a quiet achiever and all this attention got him very excited! What a guy my GM, he thought.

On the eve of the show, Helmut organised a fancy limo for Raj. After all, his Banquet Head could not travel as a Judge in an ordinary sedan.

Dressed in a smart black tuxedo, a newly purchased frilled shirt for this very occasion and a silk hand drawn bow, Raj stepped down gingerly from the limo half expecting a pretty escort to lead him from the port cochère of the club.

Where is everyone? Why am I alone? Am I too early? The card read eight pm, and here I am. This place looks spooky, what's up?

All sorts of thoughts mired his mind and suddenly from nowhere, leapt two young slim, fairylike models and purred, "Hello Mr. Raj, we were waiting for you, do come in and thank you for all your support."

This calmed Raj a bit and when both of them took an arm each of his and escorted him through the by now open night club entrance he felt *he has really arrived* in this home town of his – Penang, finally!

"A drink while we wait for the other judges?" One of them who introduced herself as Sheena, cooed. "Sure," Raj said, "why not?"

She is so kind, Raj mused.

The club looked a tad empty but would fill up for sure thought Raj. After all this was *the* Miss China Penang Show, how could it go empty?

Sheena went on to explain that the show was a bit delayed due to late arrival of a few Judges from out of town and would begin soon. "In the meantime do sit back, relax and enjoy the hospitality of the Roxanne," her musical voice resonated. Fairies they are, Raj was sure by now.

One drink followed the other in quick succession and Raj was soon viewing numerous Sheenas and Meenas around him. After some time he saw a faint image of Helmut or was it someone else? Must be someone else, Helmut was taking his wife out for a dinner he remembered even in his intensely reeling state of mind. How can Helmut be here?

A pair of warm, velvety and friendly hands soon guided Raj to the stage. "We are all set Mr. Raj," the fairy sang in his ears. Ooh… so sweetly, thought he.

"The evening has begun," someone called out, and with this the stage lit up huge, exposing a bevy of beauties who started shaking and dancing like Raj had never ever witnessed before.

Soon Raj was flung straight into their midst and found himself swaying, swirling, dancing and whistling while flashes after flashes of camera lights stormed the arena. Must be the media he thought.

Boy, am I going to be famous!

It did not take him long to sink to the floor and the next thing he remembered was being driven in an open limo all by himself, by a lady driver. He was sitting right next to her, leaning on her petite shoulder drooping like a limp morning glory.

Sometime next morning, he opened his eyes and quickly shut it tight. His head weighed a modest *ton* he thought, and his eyes wanted to part his sockets forever.

What have I done and how did I get here was all that he thought.

Late for duty for the very first time ever, Raj rushed to get dressed and sprinted from his house. Thankfully he stayed close to his workplace and managed to reach just about in time for his boss to start his morning meet.

Helmut looked up and smiled at Raj. "All went well last eve my friend?" He asked.

"Yes sir, all well," was all that Raj could muster up and say at this stage, the temples inside his head gonging louder than the bells during Thaipussam in Penang temple!

A week later Raj got married and he and Meena, his lovely demure and completely unaware of hospitality tricks-of-the-trade wife, got an invite to dine with Helmut and Julianna at their suite in the hotel.

Meena was very excited as this would be her first exposure to a luxury hotel and getting an invite from the GM was a real big deal, she thought.

That evening dressed in her best Kanjeevaram and looking like a perfectly clad newly - wed, she accompanied Raj whose pride of course, knew no bounds. Amidst jealous stares from colleagues, Raj and Meena pressed the top floor button and went up to have their first ever important dinner after their marriage at Helmut's private suite.

Helmut and Julianna were at their impeccable host's best and served Meena an exquisite vegetarian spread while Raj got to taste some of Julianna's home cooked Sarawakian seafood delicacies.

Conversation and liquor flowed smoothly and laughter rang throughout the evening. This was a happy occasion and Raj wore a proud smile on his face.

In a while, Helmut excused himself and got a small box. "Here's a gift for you Meena, please open it and tell us whether you like it."

Meena nervously unpacked the box and gasped. There lay a beautiful gold chain with a yellow coral pendant for her. What a gift she thought. What a kind man and a generous boss. Raj is so lucky and so am I.

"There is something else for you Meena." Helmut said and winked to Raj. What now? Thought Raj. One more gift, this time for me perhaps? God bless this kind soul he pondered.

Helmut handed over a beautifully wrapped album to Meena and said, "This is a surprise for you but please go through. This is what we all are and I thought you must understand the way we conduct ourselves in business sometimes. Take a hard look and tell me what you think," he said.

Meena was anxious by now and started turning the pages of the album enthusiastically.

Happiness however soon gave way to surprise and then to anger and soon tears started flowing down her cheeks endlessly. She was stunned!

Raj was everywhere, but how? Dancing, with a cigar in mouth, holding two barely clad feline like models in his two arms, spread on the ground, nestled in the bosoms of two beauties and in some pictures in such a state of happiness and ecstasy that she dared not take a second peek anymore.

Raj was in the meantime stunned too. Sitting across Meena he had not taken a look into this album, but seeing Meena so very upset, he understood that the album held the key to her misery.

Quickly he picked up the album which Meena had thrown in disgust and soon realised why she had reacted so furiously. He was trapped, all by his sweet-talking GM and his colleagues.

This was a major sting operation!

Helmut came over and consoled Meena saying all is well and this is what he thought he must explain so that the nature of our business is clear to her at the start of her marriage itself. "Raj is a good boy, he did nothing wrong," he said, "and a bit of fun does not harm anyone once in a while, does it?" He reasoned.

Raj wanted to tear his hair and explain, but who would listen? The rest of the evening was understandably icy and after coffee when Raj and Meena stepped into the lift to go back, many of his colleagues at work seemed to have a smirk hidden on the corner of their lips. Framed terribly by one and all. Everyone knows except me, he thought.

The walk back home was the most difficult one ever taken by Raj in his life. Tension was rising and Meena, just about apart from physically assaulting him, hurled the choicest tittles worthy of a maniac.

What a start off to a marriage. Is this the same Meena – my childhood sweet heart, now my wife, or is it someone else? How do I explain that I was framed!

Days at work went miserably with many a snide remark from colleagues and some extremely interested to know how the marriage was working out. Raj failed to understand as to why colleagues who hardly ever spoke to him at work now wanted to know the state of his marital life! Strange people.

It was after a week or so, Helmut walked up to Raj in his office and said, "Hey Raj, I had just gone over to your home. Did Meena call you?"

Oh no! One more surprise by Helmut. What this time? He thought. Is my marriage really a closed chapter by now?

"Relax friend, I explained everything to her and told her how we had hatched an elaborate plan to trap you. You did well though and turned out to be quite a holy soul. Good for you. I have left two passes for the real Miss China Penang tonight," he said, "do attend."

"And you are not the Judge tonight. Both of you sit back, relax and simply enjoy the show."

With this he winked at Raj and walked away!

*"It's not about making a living.
It's about living."*

Old Man and the Gun, 2018

Brand Custodians

"**Tomorrow is Sunday,** what a relief from a tough week. Let's hit town and see the latest Roger Moore release, what say?"

Sam called me from his office asking, rather declaring his intentions with great hope.

In the early part of '80s, Sam and I were posted to this very upmarket international beach resort in the South East of Asia. Fresh heads of departments were we, right after graduating from our in-company management training programme.

Hotel School students both, we were ferociously zealous in projecting the best in all what we do, trying to carve out a niche for our property as also for ourselves. No alarm clocks needed, our passions woke us up each morning. Such were we tuned then.

"Great idea," I agreed. Since tasks for the departments had almost come to a close I proposed a cup of a fresh brew coffee at the shoreline cafe managed by Alex, our friendly colleague, before calling it a day.

This was our very first posting and we were considered a bit of an outsider in this part of the world. However, since we were both single and *ready to mingle* added to the fact that we got along fabulously with the local set, learning their language enough to muster understanding and parlay pidgin versions. We enjoyed their culture and of course the local cuisine, and it really did not take long for us to be socially accepted. Or at least that is what we believed.

By the time we reached Alex's, dusk had set in and the restaurant was sparse and empty. The staff were ready to close but were happy to welcome and serve us two steaming coffees in a bit. That done, they wound up in ten and left us to enjoy the open air venue with sounds of waves lapping up the shores on a musical note.

The entire shoreline stretching miles up North to the town seemed empty except for heaped up fishing boats at intervals. Peace was all that we desired after a hectic week, in which we had hosted two back to back international residential conferences at the property.

One that of Cardiologists and the other of Archaeologists, if I recall correctly.

Sam and I shared an executive accommodation on the huge estate and since our work demanded almost day and night supervision, this suited us well.

This of course meant most of the issues pertaining to unusual requests, demands, complaints et al generally landed up on our laps and we were only too happy to take them headlong into closure. The experience of our guests remaining delighted at any cost was driven deep into our own psyche. We were determined to create wonderful and longstanding memories for them.

Sam had got up to light a smoke and headed to the empty beach for a stroll, while I was still at the deserted cafe sipping away the delightful blend.

"Hey Jim… rush," harked Sam from the nearby shoreline. "I think there's a body afloat here!"

Brand Custodians

My first reaction was as I recall, of entire disbelief. Before I could gather my thoughts I found myself on the beach with Sam inspecting a still body, face down, floating to and fro on the gentle incoming and departing waves.

Fully clothed, I distinctly remember even today, the man wore a khaki trouser and a dark striped shirt. The body was motionless, bobbing up and down, in and out of the shoreline at this time of low tide in the evening.

Sam scanned the shoreline and the cafe in a jiffy to check if there were any staff, villagers or fishermen around.

Before both of us could reason any further, Sam had turned over the body on the shore to get a closer look now. The man seemed to be a young mid-twenty person and the body possibly had swept on to our shores very recently.

Just to let you know, shorelines are not *private* as claimed by many resorts and truly as per coastal regulations they belong to the nation. True for most parts of the world, this was the case here too.

However, even as practiced today, many properties do create boundaries such that a patch is deemed private and solely for use of their guests. Not strictly cricket this, but the practice somehow continues. We were no exception frankly, and had a fish net barrier drawn up for ourselves, loosely indicating that this was indeed our very own private beach, for our sole use.

The body of the youngster was pretty much within our beach and of course within our zone therefore.

"Where do you think he belongs?" Sam queried.

Inquisitiveness got the better of me and without any forethought I hauled up his shirt collar to find out the answer. Unlike today, almost all of us then wore tailored clothing patched up with the shop details. This was a lead to find out where one would be from, I thought.

Rightly so, the tailor shop details on the stitched up patch indicated a small town up East. It was then Sam and I started debating quick alternates to tackle this unusual incident on our property.

The wisest would have definitely been to inform the Management – Security, General Manager and others, but since we were *de facto* senior management ourselves by now, for some reasons that evening we decided that we should handle this situation on our own and with stealth.

Till today I have no idea what made us do that. Our belief was so strong in our own selves that we, and none other than us, could handle this without much fuss, gave both of us an instant level of confidence and we got along to do what we now would never ever try our hands at!

"Tomorrow is Sunday," Sam whispered. "Imagine the local crowd that comes in early for swim at the adjoining beach. It will be sensational and so damaging for us if a body is found on our beach."

What bothered us then more than the issue of an unknown body was that the site was a part of the private beach of our first class hotel. Discovery of a dead body on it would give the resort guests a scare and definitely ruin our reputation.

"An international scandal and such a blot on our brand would that be!" Sam spoke aloud.

"Undoubtedly," I joined in. "I guess the safest thing to do is haul up the body. Can you see those fishing boats piled one on the other at the distant beach, Sam? Let's hide it real quick beneath those before anyone spots us."

The beach was decently dark by this time and we could not spot a single soul all along the coastline or at the resort front.

"Terrific idea," agreed Sam and immediately we got on to the task of hauling up the body – head and shoulder end by me and torso and the leg end by Sam.

The task was decided voluntarily and spontaneously by both of us I remember, such were our trust in each, never mind the guiding principles of reporting unusual incidents per operating manuals.

This was indeed a matter of protecting the image of our resort and our brand. We, the flag bearers would not let that be compromised at any cost. No way would we allow unnecessary publicity of such nature ruin our reputation, we decided.

The simple short haul of some hundred feet seemed to be an eternity that evening and once we crossed over our own beach area, we set about housing the body under the pile of upturned fishing boats.

An uncanny relief swept across me and trying to appear calm, both of us soon returned to our flat that evening. A quick shower later, we sat down to chronologically catalogue as to what had really transpired.

Was this a case of suicide? It sure did not appear like murder. Should we inform the local constabulary? We were quite friendly with them by now, theirs being a small outpost and our relations had always been cordial.

For a brief moment we agreed on informing our seniors. But soon we decided that may complicate issues. We had already done what we had to in the heat of the moment, and reporting at this stage may implicate us possibly deeper into some serious trouble.

We also by now had a local mentor, a very influential village chieftain of sorts, Tim. Apart from several businesses including fishing, water sports and others, he was also the proud owner of the county's one and only single screen theatre.

Tim was a regular at our bar each evening. We had by then got along famously such that he had even screened special midnight shows for us two, well beyond closing hours.

Should we seek his support?

Finally, both of us decided that we have taken a logical approach by shielding the body and why worry? After all we did not have a hand in this unfortunate death, suicide or murder. If at all traced back to us, and we were indeed naive to convince ourselves of that, we shall be celebrated for carrying out such a stupendous act of protecting the image of our brand.

That said, I remember we finished our dinner at the staff restaurant and tucked ourselves in, hoping to see everything sorted out the next morning.

Roger Moore's freshly released Bond movie was struck off the wish list, albeit momentarily.

By around nine the next morning, as culprits usually tend to return to the crime scene for some strange reason, we made our way back to the beach. Just to ensure that all is good.

It was not...

A decent crowd had already gathered around the fishing boats and we spotted a police jeep on the public road leading to the beach. We quickly entered our shore front restaurant and while planning a prompt exit from the *scene of the crime*, Alex the manager briskly walked in and affronted us.

"Jim, I suggest you two disappear immediately and do not be seen here today." That said, he got busy seating a fresh batch of guests who had walked in just about then.

Sam and I took the advice with alarming respect and vanished immediately to the nearby public bus stand.

Soon a bus was about to leave for the city and we promptly hopped in traveling far away from the scene of the incident.

The day was spent generally moving around one spot to the other rather listlessly, and we realised that both of us did not have the appetite to go in for our eagerly awaited Roger Moore release. Post lunch at our favourite Lobster Shack in town, we headed back, fervently hoping that by now the uproar would have subsided at the resort.

This time round we headed straight for our flat.

Next morning back to the hotel for work we had our ears up and eyes open, looking for signs of any development or news of the dead body and someone nailing us for it. Perhaps someone had noticed without us being aware.

Our meets with the General Manager and other Heads of Departments in the following couple of months or so went off relatively bland. In the sense that we were neither quizzed nor there surfaced a reference to the incident on the beach.

This did give us reprieve and satisfaction that our heroic endeavour had indeed saved the resort and company some unnecessary, undue publicity. I guess at that age, this was our own way of cheering for our own selves as *brand custodians* and this served us as a huge self-motivation, a job well done.

Soon relieved with time we forgot about the whole episode. Did this smug happiness last for long?

It surely did not.

One morning the phone rang.

Precisely at around noon, I still remember the time even after so many years, Sam called me up.

"Jim," he said, "we have been summoned to the local police station. Just you and me, right away."

With my heart literally in mouth, I queried, "Did you spurt something out? What did they say?"

"Relax, they have just asked us to come in briefly and let me assure you no one in the resort knows so far. The day is a bit relaxed, so let's do a make-belief joint inspection of the exit area cottages. Then we can reach the outpost from around the staff quarters," he chipped in.

"Anyways," he added, "it is Alf, the Inspector, your pal. It's he who called."

Yes indeed, Alf was an amiable individual and during his routine rounds of our huge estate, had become friendly with us, sharing rounds of coffee once in a while. Friendship to that extent only and nothing beyond, truly.

Both of us presented ourselves to the station which was a small outpost in between multiple resorts located on the widespread beach. Factually this was a Tourist Police Outpost, not a heavily staffed office and definitely not housed with seniors adept at handling serious crime.

Alf greeted us pleasantly. "Coffee?" He offered, trying to return our regular hospitality at the resort, I guess.

"Gentlemen, are you aware of a body that had got washed onto our shores some couple of months ago?" He asked.

Both of us now sure that he was trying to connect some dots around the incident that evening, had no choice, but to answer in the affirmative.

"I am trying to close the investigation today as we have been able to track the family in his home town, interstate – mind it, and this has been established as a case of suicide now."

"Did you notice anyone hovering around your beach area that evening or maybe the early morning next, showing interest in the body or anything else you could fill us in with?"

"I have been inquiring from staff of other resorts too, but not been able to gather anything substantial. Was there an accomplice or a few friends with him that day when this occurred or was it indeed washed onto this beach from somewhere else? Any recollection would help," he asked of us.

By now Sam and I were totally convinced that someone must have noticed us and possibly tipped the police. This is how this call from the station landed up. Deep terror had struck in by then and somehow managing a cool facade we gave him a blank stare, suggesting a negative.

Alf stared at us deep and for long, in the end somehow deciding not to quiz us further.

Our coffee on his table by this time had died untasted.

Bidding farewell, he promised to catch up soon at our café for a snack and chat about latest movie releases. Oh yes, I forgot to mention, he was quite a movie buff too, much like both of us.

Relieved, we went back to our duties and life, and this matter was never brought up ever until…

Tim was the owner of our local movie theatre, the single theatre around for miles and a regular to our bar at the resort, as I mentioned earlier.

Soon we had got along eminently and believe it or not, influential as he was, he was a friend of friends.

Often, he would screen special shows well beyond the late night timings just for close buddies as Sam and I and as you would have guessed – for Alf from our Tourist Police Outpost.

This used to be a major high for us bachelors and Tim was a great host too, treating us with some amazing short eats and fresh brews during the shows.

One evening Sam got a call. "What are you both up to this eve? Join me for a special screening of the latest Roger Moore film. My family is coming in too," invited Tim.

Excited, and more so since we had missed that film in our previous outing, we landed up.

Halfway into the super film, Tim suddenly shot a volley at me straight. "So how did your inquest into the beach incident go down my friend? All cool?"

So, this was it…

Tim would have been wired some information and possibly it was he who made sure that we two *innocent* friends do not get framed for apparently abetting no crime whatsoever.

Thankful as hell, I chose not to reply and continued watching the action on screen while concentrating on the bowl of prawn fritters in front of me.

Sadly, I don't recollect the second half of the exciting film anymore!

I must watch it once again. Very soon I have decided - on OTT…

*"Wait a minute, wait a minute.
You ain't heard nothing yet."*

The Jazz Singer, 1928

The Case of the Missing Guest

Nightfall happened quite early that evening.

Normally, on our equatorial island guarded heavily on the West and North by lush tropical forest the sun casts it's hues late, until almost quarter to eight in the evening, year round.

Overcast skies and a steady drizzle had followed since early evening. Under the protective shade of our seaside bar, my wife, a few friends who had come visiting us and were staying at the resort, and I were catching up after a day's work.

It was close to three years that I was posted on this rainforest island resort in the South East.

I had by now if I could say, a good hold on the layout of our large five-hundred-acre island resort cum marina and quite a decent knowledge of the vast forest area that surrounded us.

The day had been reasonably busy and as this was the start of the school holiday season, we were getting quite a few families coming in to stay. Most families were spending their leisure time enjoying water sports, lazing on our different beaches, hosting family barbeques and generally catching up precious lost time with their loved ones.

Experienced hotel staff would know what to do when families come in for holidays. Touch base, get to know their desires, organise that to perfection and of course take care of needs of their children to the fullest. It is mostly for children that families come in, and keeping them happy surely means a lot including word of mouth and therefore repeat business.

Mr. and Mrs. Ong from Jakarta had checked in the same morning and with them were their two very well-behaved children, a son and a daughter, both teenagers. I remember they were assigned a ground floor two bed villa which overlooks one part of our forest and the other the main beach.

I had got to meet them during their check-in and later got busy with one or the other work that came up. I presumed like most other families, they would have gone ahead with their plans of a well - deserved family holiday and were being looked after by our team.

But not all wishes get granted…

Around seven p.m. Anwar, our efficient Front Office Manager, came up and asked me to be excused from the group as I had an important call waiting at the lobby.

This when done by a colleague in our trade, without fail means something serious has come up and one is being given a forewarning – albeit discreetly.

"For the past hour we have been looking for Mrs. Ong of Villa 207. She was last reported to be seen in her room around five p.m. by the family and seems to have simply vanished shortly after that."

"At quarter to six Mr. Ong reported this to us and we have been searching high and low but now with lights failing and few areas remaining to be searched I thought of bringing this to your notice."

Anwar had done the right thing. He had tried to conduct a search mission himself with his team and when unsuccessful, flashed it to his senior. Troubling as it was, since the island was really huge with possibilities of even getting lost in our forests (*which a few guests had in the past*), we discussed our options swiftly. It was decided to bring in the Emergency Response Team or ERT for short into action.

Primarily the equivalent of the SWAT team of the resort, ERT consisted of resident staff members mainly pulled in from our dedicated Gurkha Security Team and headed by the Security Manager. This crack outfit is routinely trained in fire-fighting, search and rescue, high seas evacuation, tsunami alert and assistance and handling of snakes and reptiles, primates etc., among many other important duties in keeping the various residents on the island safe and secure.

Playing Sherlock Holmes however, is not their forte…

"Let us get the team together Anwar. Let's form at least four search teams and start operations on main beach, secondary beach, West side and forest areas to start with," I requested.

Soon armed with torches, ropes, first-aid boxes and other search and rescue essentials four teams were dispatched by Anwar to respective locations. In the meantime my wife, few others and I went over to visit the family at their ground floor chalet to dig in further.

"We were all inside the room playing in the living area when my wife went into the bedroom and shut the door," informed Mr. Ong.

He seemed calm and composed and I felt an instant awe for this person who seemed to have gathered himself well despite this recent trauma.

The children seemed calm too but I supposed that would be more in the hope that their mother would reappear any time now.

"When she did not appear close to fifteen minutes, I entered the bedroom and found the windows wide open. It is then that I started my search and went over to look for her in the other bedrooms and bath. She was not there as well. I realised she could have jumped out of the open window. I then called Anwar and informed him. That was around six p.m., it is close to seven thirty now."

Soon we went outside and carried out, as I recall, a thorough search of the periphery and beneath the raised wooden chalet just to make sure that the lady is not hiding there or fallen and hurt herself, hoping she is present somewhere around.

The drizzle by now had turned more than that and any chance that we could have traced some footprints on this slushy ground leading straight into the forest behind the wooden chalet by then, was a no-go.

All this while, our ERT were going up and down their respective areas of search. Information continuously streamed on walkie talkies indicating no sighting of the lady so far.

It was time to inform the local police, I thought. In our business it is imperative that the constabulary, senior police officials, government, para government machinery, medical and other fraternity are well networked as ours' is a public service business.

We called the local station and informed them that perchance we fail to trace the lady, we may need their assistance. Insofar as this island is concerned it so happens that the geography is largely known to whole timer residents as us, therefore, it is better we attempt first before requesting any outside force, I reckoned.

While all this was on, my wife who often chips in voluntarily to assist us in our operational work was seen comforting the children.

The daughter was a bit shy but the boy appeared more confident and soon enough started chatting up with her on their school, hobbies and friends.

"When there is unhappiness in the house this is what happens," suddenly this under toned remark from the son came by.

"I believe there is something more to this affair, let me dig out. We may come to know more," my wife said, and got chatting with the children even more intimately.

Mr. Ong, in the meantime, was on his smoke and looked pretty collected. A bit strange for someone whose wife has been missing for some time now, I now thought.

With the family taken care of, I decided to join one of my teams who were on the far off beach, a fair distance away from the main resort area – more to keep the team motivated and add on one more hand to the mission.

Taking a battery-operated buggy, our most trusted vehicle for all purposes, I sped off to the area and by this time, let me add, darkness had completely set in. It was pitch dark and past eight now with rain showing no signs of abatement.

By the time I reached the second beach I found the entire team of Gurkhas, led by Anwar and one youngster from our Sports Activities Department – Zul, returning back.

"What report team?" I asked. "No luck chief, but we have something else to tell you," said Zul. He pulled me aside appearing visibly shaken.

"Quickly turn back, we have a *Hantu* following us and for god's sake don't look back," he pleaded.

Zul informed that the search for about an hour on this beach, its surrounding areas and an old unused site nearby yielded no result at all. On their return via the forest Anwar was the last man in file, Zul one ahead of him and leading them were four Gurkhas. On one bend Zul turned around to speak to Anwar. It was then, that he saw this silhouette of a woman in white, trailing Anwar.

Let me add, the concept of *Hantu* or spirits is widely recognised in many parts of the world and hugely here as well. Our island is said to house an old man *Orang Hijau* or man in green, who is revered as the guardian spirit of the place. While most have seen him, my sheer bad luck he has always chosen to evade me even on my nightly routine rounds of the island. Maybe he just doesn't appreciate my presence, I always believed!

Coming back, the idea of a lady in white trailing Anwar who chose to appear to Zul but not to Anwar, and her reappearance after another bend according to Zul, seemed to take the winds of some of the otherwise strong-willed Gurkhas too.

I was a bit unfazed at this stage but this got me thinking. What if this was the same missing lady herself playing hide and seek with our team?

With this in mind we spent another fifteen minutes scouting the area but this turned to be completely futile and confused us even more. Finally we decided to reconvene our rescue teams from all corners for a quick debrief and to decide upon the next plan. We soon met up at the main security outpost.

"All right team, what have we got?" I asked. "Negative", was the response from all fronts. The West side team had explored the whole South to West face of the island, the main beach area team had done the same with the main beach face and adjoining areas. Part of the forest areas were also rummaged around by another team as it was practically impossible to enter the deep forests in this inclement weather now.

"Ideas please gentlemen," I requested. Frankly I was quickly running out of ideas myself. This, by now a three-hour search and rescue mission has yielded no concrete results, except that we had been followed by a white veiled spirit!

Mildly frightening but more frustrating I thought.

"We continue our efforts and hold on the police arrival. In fact, they would not be of much help as firstly it is dark, secondly our areas are better known by us than any outsider," advised one of the associates. Accepting this we went back to our jobs of looking after other guests and left two teams now to continue the search and giving us updates.

Returning to the main resort area reception I had an excited team waiting for me.

"Did you find any clues? I promise you will not. There is more to this story, let me fill you in," my wife whispered enthusiastically.

Summarising what she had gathered from the children, it appeared that Mr. and Mrs. Ong had a huge tiff early on in the day.

Believing he was alone, Mr. Ong was happily chatting with one of his girl friends on mobile near our main beach describing in tantalising details the beauty of the island and the romantic location.

"We must come back here darling and spend some intimate time. I promise I shall bring you here very soon," Mr. Ong was assuring.

Little did he realise that Mrs. Ong had in the meantime crept up from behind with an idea of giving company to her *faithful* husband. Instead she got to listen to every bit of this saucy conversation.

Filled with fury, it appears she had snatched the mobile from her husband who by now was a figure of a statue frozen in ice, too stunned by this sudden turn of events. Before he could realise, the carrier of promiscuous conversation was dispatched to the depths of the sea – a burial befitting it's traitorous deed!

So much so for the family holiday. The rest of the day was spent in sullen moments and by evening this final episode of disappearance.

Incidentally it was not the first case of leaving abode. Mrs. Ong had left home once earlier too and did attempt suicide on a couple of occasions because of the husband's philandering habits.

"When there is unhappiness in the house this is what happens." This one off remark now suddenly made more sense to me.

Women of course make better sleuths, I immediately concluded. Our very own *Miss Marple* had all along smelt something fishy.

With so much information and our lady still not in sight we still had no wrap up yet. While it was completely inappropriate to discuss personal life issues with guests, with this *intel* in hand I felt we had hope.

Leaving home for Mrs. Ong has been more than a one-time affair. In the back of our minds we felt we will find her soon and hoped that we should do it by break of day, at least.

"If she has attempted suicide before and that she is still alive, rest assured she will be alive now as well," reassured Anwar.

By this time it was closing in to eleven at night a clear five hours of complete disappearance of the lady from our midst.

Anwar, my wife and I had just settled in to our restaurant and were considering a bite when we found two of our guards rushing towards Mr. Ong's chalet.

"Looks like there has been a breakthrough," Anwar excitedly commented. Sure enough, by the time we got there we found our guards carrying the missing lady back to the room.

It appears she was found crouching outside behind her room, in the open, beneath the window and when two of our guards had gone back to search, they found her. She apparently fainted seeing them and they in turn informed others.

Now this is the same spot where we had personally done extensive search to start with!

The adjoining area is totally *forested* and it is quite nerve shackling to enter even during day leave alone at night with a steady downpour to top it all. So how and where did she actually manage to vanish and hide for a good five hours is a mystery to us even today.

Mrs. Ong was made to settle down and our team organised some warm milk for her. My wife entered her room and this is what she subsequently gathered from discussions with her.

The lady admitted she had jumped out of the window but that she was asked by someone else to do so. A woman who beckoned her from outside the window.

A lady in white!

Beyond this she claimed she had no recollection of what transpired and that she only recalls two men flashing torch on her face. That is when she fainted.

Did she go inside the forest? She does not remember. Did she go beneath the vast empty space of the chalets – she does not remember. Did she go to any other area of the resort in the darkness – other beach areas? She has no remembrance.

A pretty strange case this. Who was this woman who beckoned her? She does not know. Neither do we. Was it the same woman who was trailing Anwar in a white silhouette? We will never know.

In the meantime, my wife and the lady had warmed up and I heard her counsel both Mr. and Mrs. Ong on good matrimonial relationship matters among other small talk.

I have no idea how much ice that would cut in their family life but I sincerely wished that it did, especially for the sake of the children who were indeed very poised during this whole trauma.

Beyond my scope of professional duties, I chose to of course keep out of this advisory council!

As in ERT language we now *stood down,* and since the episode had come to a happy close we retreated.

Wishing the family a very good night I thanked all members of the team who were mighty relieved as well, after a good five hour run this evening in wet and inhospitable environment.

A guard was discreetly placed at a distance and advised to keep a watch on the chalet with routine patrols just in case we have a sequel coming up!

Anwar our efficient Front Desk Manager promptly got down to officially record the incident and thus ended the strange episode of our *missing guest*.

Mr. Ong and family left the following day cutting short their holiday, a loss of revenue indeed for our resort.

My wife and I were there specially to wish them *Zaijian* and a very happy life…

"What we've got here is a failure to communicate."

Cool Hand Luke, 1967

Black Dog

Rao was the trusted and most efficient of the Banquet waiters that we had in our hotel.

Situated in Bangalore (now Bengaluru) in the eighties this was the place to be. The rich and the famous, the glamorous film crowd, the paparazzi, political wheeler dealers of various hues all loved this place, and we were busy year- round.

Bangalore during Derby and other racing competition hosted the country's poshest prize winning events and that the city was a liquor hub did help a lot too.

Many of the country's beer and liquor manufacturers had production units in and around Bangalore and many owners even today reside here. Undoubtedly they also monopolise the Bangalore races so to say with their prize winning horses and jockeys, while playing major sponsors for many a lavish after event revelry.

Somewhat a tradition, come racing season, all the owners along with their jockeys and the glam entourage would throng our hotel. Post races we would be busy with multiple celebratory gatherings hosted by the winners for their friends and business associates.

The atmosphere would be electric and liquor flowing like a river in spate. No expense was small or spared to lay out exceptional and exotic cuisine embellished with matching wines and spirits. All in all, the events were truly divine, and the hotel enjoyed spoiling their guests with their perfected routine of unobtrusive service.

This yearly ritual had become a custom and it was at such functions that Mr. Rao, the Banqueting Captain, excelled at his art of service with a do - or - die attitude which so impressed those who he had selected for his attention and favour.

The selection of course was diligently made. Those who did not qualify to be elite enough to be attended by his own *royal* touch and also among them who were suspect of being parsimonious, would naturally find themselves relegated from the list of *illuminati of the eve*.

The chosen few would have his undivided attention and the free loaders or guests with lower credentials would have to make do with other waiting staff without having the benefit of even a glance from the *suave* Rao Sahib.

Each guest was aware that such royal attention had an unwritten contract which cannot be rescinded or repealed at any stage and would end only with the most attractive gratuity to Rao.

This art of the master, many in his own team and some from other outlets wanted to capture and make their own. Rao was blessed with a sixth sense too, not only did he have a great memory he also had the sense of anticipation of a need. Even if such a need did not arise, he could quickly turn it into a suggestion and present it to the guest as a favour.

With such artifice he would tend to every wish and desire of his patrons that they had become habituated to his indulgences. His list of services extended to and beyond the immediate menu to food that was curated especially for his *honourable* guests by our kitchens without contest.

How he could manage such feats was indeed amazing. However, our singular objective was to keep guests delighted prompting Managers and Chefs to intervene sometimes on behalf of Rao for a favour or two from their own staff!

The waiters especially the older ones were in awe of him but would only show contempt as they had not the alacrity to handle guest demands with the finesse that Rao possessed. He in his own right was an inspirational figure for the younger inexperienced waiters while the senior waiters privately hated him.

Rao's do or die attitude took him beyond the boundaries of his authority many a times of which he had very little of in the first place, but he was at such events either blind to this fact or purposely oblivious. One could say he was the de facto *Concierge of the Hotel* and a Banquet waiter at the same time. The Hotel Management was also aware of the magic of Rao and would sometimes turn a blind eye to his exploits. After all the bouquet of formal compliments went always to the Management from the desks of the CEO or owners post such events.

However, every king is put to a test and so was *King Rao*...

As things would have it, two rival liquor barons were hosting separate functions one evening and we were exceptionally busy taking care of our large number of corporate and other guests at these venues.

Our Hotel GM was at the lobby and in the tradition of hoteliers had positioned himself strategically, busy welcoming and shaking hands with various celebrities as they arrived.

My Banquet section was split into two teams – one at the pool side where a party was in progress and another in our main massive and beautiful Ball Room.

Rao had taken upon a dual role to play today. He was soon observed serving, clearing, replenishing drinks and snacks to his *illuminati* to perfection at both the functions. Though this was not officially scheduled for him…

One would notice him at the pool side busy as a bee serving the host as polite as would make deference die of shame, and the next moment at the Ball Room where the other Baron would discover that he was mightier than he hitherto had imagined himself to be.

Flexing amazing reflexes all in the name of service, but with a hawk like eye kept out so that the next drink is truly replenished by he and he only and no one else, Rao was on a roll.

In between I would spot him organising *out of menu* delicacies from our French restaurant and in the next from our very popular Asian, only for his chosen *noble* customers.

How he did that and with whose authority was not ours' to ask as long as our guests were happy. Rao was truly a master fixer.

Both the functions were proceeding well when all of a sudden I got a message that there was a complaint by the main host of the party taking place at the poolside.

"Where is Rao?" Liquor baron *numero uno* thundered at me.

"Just a moment sir, let me fetch him for you. I saw him serving you a moment ago."

"Yes, he took my order and has vanished. Can you do something about refilling my glass young man?"

That done, I went off to hunt for Rao. This was most un - Rao like to leave an important guest without delivering his order and vanish, I mused.

I scouted for Rao for a good ten minutes, questioning all my colleagues and when I was about to give up, I decided to call on the Security Control room staff.

Now, these were pre CCTV days and the only way you could locate where one is within the estate was by either calling up a department on phone, or physically launching a search yourself.

Even our security would do the same, starting with the staff entry - exit gate which would be one area that would keep a written log of anyone coming in or going out of the premise.

Sure enough, Lal Bahadur, our ever vigilant security guard on duty informed Rao had indeed landed up there, opened his jacket and handed over to him in a great hurry. He then had vanished on his Vespa to somewhere just about ten minutes ago.

He was being sent on an important mission by liquor baron *numero uno* so he has no time to sign off, he had added while speeding off on his scooter.

Having no idea where this conversation was leading to and in no mood to catch up with the important yet irate host at the poolside any time soon, I decided to hang around and wait for Rao to find out about his disappearing act.

While I was debating various scenarios in my mind as to what would have happened and what plausible revert I would offer baron *numero uno,* in around five minutes I saw Rao speeding in his on his scooter and what appeared to me, with two black mongrel puppies cushioned neatly in a basket on the pillion riders seat.

The puppies were yelping merrily and seemed to be enjoying a ride of their lifetime.

Completely puzzled I waited for Rao to alight, who by now was convincing Lal Bahadur to hand over his waiter's jacket and permit him to enter the hotel with these two puppies.

"Rao, are you nuts?" I asked. "You vanish from your duty without permission and now want to get back inside the hotel with these puppies in hand? What is the issue?"

"Boss, believe me I was asked to get them by our host," he said.

"Impossible."

"Honest," pleaded Rao. "The guest asked me to get him a black dog. Next to the staff quarters I have seen these two black puppies since last week. See I always aim to please, I got him two instead! Now please allow me. He will be upset if I did not follow his orders."

So, this was it, the whole thing now turned clear!

Black Dog, the Scotch (whisky) was just launched that very week in India and it was getting mighty fashionable for the *hoi polloi* to call for it in public. Showed off their status you see!

Our hotel had still not got its consignment of this brand and therefore we were not serving it yet.

Rao unfortunately had no idea about the fact that the order for a Black Dog was truly for a whisky.

This is what our guest would have called for (in a reasonably loud and flashy manner I am sure) and Rao ever eager to please, now stood with two small puppies in his hands having fished them out from our neighbourhood.

I wondered whether the *mother doggy* would take it kindly when Rao went to return her babies.

Ingenious as it may be, you have guessed it right, there was no way Rao got permission to serve this unique order!

Black Dog Scotch landed up soon on our shelves and till today whenever I look at a bottle of this lovely nectar, I cannot help but remember Rao, the original – *never say no* person…

*"I'm mad as hell,
and I'm not going to take it
anymore."*

Network, 1976

Found and Lost

"Habibi, I want to see the General Manager right now!"

Distraught written all over his face pleaded the guest, staying at our hotel for the past two days, on his honeymoon.

Suzilan, the Duty Manager of this downtown uber luxury property was an old hand at the hotel. Handling irate customers with ease and professionalism was his hallmark. For all new entrants in the Front Office he was the chosen departmental trainer as well.

Suzilan immediately took the guest to a quieter area of the lobby and tried to understand the situation while pacifying the guest. A past master of handling difficult situations, he was *hotelier par excellence*.

Listen, Empathise, Apologise and Act were key principles that he always practiced and immediately got down to understanding what the guest was upset about.

"I have lost my new wife, my friend" blurted the guest.

Stunned at this novel lost and found complaint, Suzilan dumbfounded as he was, quickly composed himself and tried to console the guest as professionally as he could.

He swished out his buzzer and requested the Security Head to come right away to the lobby where he was.

In a moment he was joined by Zain the Security Head, and both of them got down to asking details of this strange case of a partner missing on their honeymoon.

"What sort of a hotel is this? You must find my wife. It is your responsibility," blamed the guest passing the ball of ownership of the problem squarely on the shoulders of the hotel.

"Let's get some facts on the case sir and we will surely help you. Right now please calm down and do cooperate," implored Suzilan.

"Incompetent management you have here. If you do not sort this out in the next half hour I will call the police," the guest now threatened, his voice rising quite a few decibels.

Now no decent hospitality establishment wishes to get undue and negative publicity or have police ramble around their public areas. That is not desirable and can create a hugely negative PR value in the market, surely to be exploited by the cut throat competition.

Suzilan proceeded, "When did you see her last sir?"

"We were in the room after dinner last night. I dined at the French Brasserie in your hotel and by ten or so we were both off to bed," he said.

"Then what happened?" Asked Zain the Security Head.

"What do you mean? We went off to sleep." The guest replied, visibly irritated.

"At around eleven she was there on bed. I got up at about two in the morning and then I looked at the other side of the bed and she was missing! I searched our suite and balcony, nook and cranny but she was just not there. I came down to your coffee shop, lounge and searched and still did not find her. I went back and slept then. I was sure she will land up soon, I thought." he said.

"How strange? How can a person vanish from your reputed hotel? Your responsibility now completely to find her," he demanded.

This was getting to be around ten in the morning so the lady had vanished for a cool eight hours, Suzilan calculated.

Zain promised to have a property round of the hotel with the guest and Suzilan got down to now checking all CCTV recordings in the control room with a senior security supervisor. Just to track any leads to this strange encounter of a guest missing from the premises.

Half an hour into the check, Suzilan saw a strange footage.

In the wee hours at around quarter to two out comes a burkha clad lady from the guest lift 'A' into the lobby. She steps out, looks right and left with caution and proceeds to the ladies restroom located nearby.

Ten minutes later an unveiled beauty with trendy make up, wearing a fashionable jeans and a tank top, clutching a fancy Louis Vuitton handbag is spotted rushing towards the lobby exit.

Suzilan requested the supervisor for camera recording to now focus on the lobby exit door no. three and lo and behold, at timer showing 02:07:07 this pretty lady is joined by another handsome fellow waiting for him at the port cochére.

They exchange smiles, give each other a hug and is soon hailed a cab by our very own doorman on duty.

Off they go and now there is no doubt where this lost and found story has led to!

Found and Lost | 65

To keep matters under cover, Suzilan called the guest now to the control room and asked Zain to explain what had happened.

"Do you wish to see the recording sir?"

"Sure, please go ahead," came the eager reply.

By the time the camera recording spectacle ended poor Mr. Mohammed, our guest, had his head tucked into his hands and was weeping uncontrollably.

He just kept on pouring and pouring! Now this was another situation...

He obviously loved her so very much.

"Why? Why?" He kept asking.

Obviously, the hotel team had no answer.

Suzilan and Zain kept silent for a while and when things got a bit under control the guest declared, "I want to check out Habibi."

"I will go report this matter to our Embassy," he said. "Thank you for all your support and if you find the man who stole my wife please contact me," he pleaded.

Later investigations by security revealed that the lover boy too had housed himself in the same hotel and the plot must have been an old one, obviously hatched by the duo sometime back.

So, while Suzilan and Zain could manage to solve this strange lost and *almost* found case, what happened to poor Mr. Mohammed or the runaway lovers was never reported back, *for reasons completely understandable...*

"Houston, we have a problem."

Apollo 13, 1995

Close Encounter

Our guest list boasted some very senior captains of the industry. Balwantji was one of them. A very pleasant person, he was undoubtedly the darling of our hotel staff.

In his early 40's, Balwant was a regular to our property where I was a newbie at the Front Desk having just finished my hotel school education.

Balwant visited us for short duration stays frequenting at least twice a month. If there was a survey for selecting the most loved and adored guest of our hotel, Balwant would have won hands down. So popular was he!

Centrally located in Kolkata flanked by host of iconic heritage restaurants and bars, our seasoned hands at Front Desk as Banerjee-da, Manmeet et al were often hosted by Balwant in these establishments of repute quite regularly.

These favours were time and again returned, I could see, by upgrades to luxury suites, special welcome amenities, preferential seating at our restaurants, and of course a whole lot of touches and offerings otherwise provided to should I say, someone as senior as a designated Head of State!

I was getting to be, in the meantime, an able assistant to the old timers and once in a way allowed to handle shifts alone. Ad interim, they would be practicing *customer centricity* by joining our dear guests as Balwant in the various eateries and watering holes or later as I learnt, even joining some for a day at the races!

Our favourite guest Balwantji was a much married man and lived in Delhi which was his home. But our hotel was no less, a home away from home, I mean. For him.

Balwant had a regular visitor – a *friend* let us say, a lady of course, during his stays with us. This was an affair which all staff knew but rarely discussed.

Privacy of guests was something that was zealously guarded by the team. As I have mentioned, the *quid pro quo* payoffs seemed to maintain that veil very well. On occasions when Mrs. Balwant accompanied him, of course there was no visit from the *friend* and I noticed that none of our seniors were invited out for their *customer engagement* meeting and luncheons.

On one weekend eve towards the end of a winter month, I remember Balwantji walking in and Manmeet, our senior supervisor in Front Office, doing an express check-in for him, leaving all other matters immediately to my disposition.

He escorted Balwant to the room personally and in a bit came down, settling his favourite guest of all times.

"Take care, Balwantji's *friend* would be here soon, make sure she is guided to our guest's room pronto!" He commanded.

"Yes boss, will be done," I said and got down to my duties.

Presently in walked a petite persona, the lady friend of Bawant, a known socialite, and got down to pleasantries with Manmeet.

In a moment, instead of me, Manmeet took the guest lift with her and went up to Balwant's room. Our guest would surely be most eagerly waiting for his other love of life by now.

I was sort of relieved I did not have to do this. Immersing myself in left over jobs of Manmeet and Banerjee-da, I frantically completed the remaining clerical works so that the evening duty hand over runs smooth sans melee.

So far so good and the shift went off uneventfully with nothing much to write home about. No fracas, no demanding clients, no maintenance issues or complaints of other departments to take note of and resolve.

The next day was my weekly off and I was already in a happy mode debating in my mind whether I should see the latest Amitabh release again or go for a popular play at *theatre para* with my friends.

Just as we were moving off shift and the graveyard fellows were waiting to take over, in walked Mrs. Balwant.

All eyes immediately got trained on madam and incoming as well as the outgoing shift team, both, literally stood frozen! There was no heads up about her visit this time round!

Manmeet was carrying out shift duties of cash and I saw him stop all work, shut the cash desk, rollover the cash handover register and literally dash out to greet Mrs. Balwant.

"Good evening madam, what a pleasant surprise and so happy to see you. Welcome back to your home. Bhai Gurung handle madam's baggage immediately," he cooed in his most courteous, hospitable and honey moulded tone.

Gurung, our old and reliable Page Boy was as stunned as everyone else and quite forgetting his duties for the time, with his jaw partially opened, was staring at Mrs. Balwant who had walked in with one piece of a luggage all by herself.

Hearing Manmeet's orders he jumped back to the moment and gave his flashiest smile relieving madam of her luggage and greeted her.

"Welcome back madam, what a pleasure to have you back, let me handle your bag," purred he.

Mrs. Balwant was herself a svelte figure, and generally open to flattery and bolstering of her ego, something which many of our staff were past masters of. Manmeet by then, we all saw, had started chatting with her right at the lobby hoping to engage her in small talk while figuring out what do next.

Our lobby veered out to the hotel's 24 hour All Day Diner and Manmeet quickly suggested with all the grace at his command, "Madam, lovely to have you after so long. Chaliye let's have a nice cup of your favourite masala chai to celebrate the occasion or catch up on a spot of dinner before we lose your charming company to sir!"

Saying this in a honey twilled tone and giving practically no opportunity for her say no, he escorted her gallantly to our Coffee Shop leading the way smoothly.

To Gurung he ordered, "Gurung bhai don't get the luggage yet to the room. Let ma'am give sir a surprise," and with this he gave him a quick wink and a nod.

Gurung got the message loud and clear and vanished promptly as would the genie from his lamp.

By this time our favourite guest was informed by the other gurus of our front desk of the arrival of the real lady of the house and that she was being currently engaged by Manmeet at the Coffee Shop.

Later on as confirmed by our able housekeeping staff what followed next was utter haplessness, confusion and panic

by our guest, totally confounded as what to do next and how to save the day and perhaps his life thereafter.

"Hai ab kya hoga, main to barbad ho gaya, yeh kaise hua," were his constant lament. *I am finished* - he kept wailing. Scantily clad as he was with his muse on similar dress levels he kept circling his room, round and round, muttering all to himself, again and again. "Oye ab kaise bachenge, yeh kaise hua," and such pitiful cries kept repeatedly escaping his lips!

Perplexed and harassed, our favourite guest it appeared was on a state of complete nervous breakdown.

Gurung had by this time taken charge and the first thing he did was a quick evacuation of the *lady friend* via the fire exit stairs and then out via the staff exit gate. He ensured she was hailed a taxi and safely couriered out of the periphery of our hotel.

He then instructed the housekeeping staff to do a prompt super VIP room clean up, ensuring that double amenities for both husband and wife were stocked up right away.

Next he called up the F&B and asked them to immediately dispatch the freshest of madam's favourite fruits and cookies on a silver platter and informed the Pastry section to do up a large chocolate truffle cake with *Welcome Back* piped on it.

Dry fruits from the Pantry and an expensive French Champagne in an ice cooler was organised at neck breaking efficiency and the room cleared out of any tell - tale evidences.

Aired out and freshened, this was a fifteen minute super hustle.

Close Encounter

All this time Balwantji had parked himself on the living room sofa of his suite looking at the operation with confusion, awe and ultimate deep appreciation of the team.

He quickly freshened up and was now ready to receive his wife who was to give him a surprise, except now instead, he would give her one!

Manmeet in the meantime was running out of stories and small talk while Mrs. Balwant too a tad tired of listening to a hotel staff's yarn. Her mind was now solely focused on meeting her husband and retiring for the day.

Gurung by now appeared back on the scene and got immensely busy polishing cutlery, helping out the Coffee Shop staff, a work which was completely out of his job description.

Manmeet got the message that things are sorted and turned and asked me to personally carry the luggage, escorting madam to the third floor suite. I did this flawlessly wondering how Balwant would react on seeing his wife.

I rang the doorbell and out came Balwantji. His broad smile (of relief I thought) said it all.

"What a surprise darling! Should have told me, would have come to airport my dear, to pick you up," he sung. Embracing her and quickly escorting her inside, he relieved me of her bag while tucking in a large gratuity into my coat pocket.

Of course, the surprise visit turned out to be a grand welcome instead and she was thrilled to bits seeing the room made up so invitingly for her, I was told later.

Tales of a Hotelwallah

I wished them a very good night and a happy stay and since this chapter closed for the time being successfully, I came down to attend to my work.

All's well that ends well. I supposed.

At the front desk however, the tip amount was promptly released of me by my seniors. They felt they had done bulk of the hard job, saving private and intimate details of our hotel's beloved guest and pulling off this orchestrated operation with precision. So they deserved it, was their logic.

Hierarchy prevailed and there was no debating such argument with seniors. It was time to go home anyway.

I was on a weekly off the next day and got to hear the proceedings on reporting back for work on the following rostered shift.

Mrs. Balwant had checked out late next evening and flown back to Delhi, after a delightful stay peppered with lavish pampering of our hotel staff, and tender love and care by her husband.

Balwant had thanked the staff profusely and later gifted all front desk and other staff individually with packets of serious bank notes.

He too had checked out the very next day and flew back to Delhi.

This time we got to keep our share thankfully. I was handed mine by Manmeet personally.

The whole episode left a casualty though… The Hotel!

Balwantji shifted his preference of stay and never visited us again.

We missed him. Most of all, Manmeet…

Close Encounter | 75

*"Fasten your seatbelts.
It's going to be a bumpy night."*

All About Eve, 1950

Just Another Day

The hills beckoned us now with a fresh posting and as advised by our company, Sandhya and I packed ourselves out to this lovely destination of lakes, waterfalls and scenic surroundings.

I was to be a first time General Manager and indeed this called for to put my best foot forward. Sandhya, apart from being my partner in life was also an executive with the company and she was to look after the Rooms Division as it's Head.

This state capital was generally visited by business folks and visiting out of state bureaucracy, but not really till then seen much of tourists as a segment of traffic.

When I moved in, the property needed immense operational and upkeep support. It was at best managed quite like a *sarkari* guest house – not a professional hotel, in senses that we know of in hospitality.

We moved into our allotted suite and settled in as soon as we could, trying to tidy up affairs. I recall the festive period saw us doing a grand X'mas and a New Year's celebration, bringing in much needed revenues and appreciation, both.

It turned out to be the first such celebration in the property and created a decent buzz in the town for the hotel and all of us.

The fateful night

Woken up by sounds of loud banging on our suite's door, I opened it and in barged six masked intruders. Two of these ruffians immediately negotiated my arms and started raining blows and kicks in harsh quick succession. Alarmed at the unwarranted onslaught, Sandhya who had by now rushed in from the bedroom to the en-suite living room, started wailing, "Stop bhaiyyas, you will kill him!"

By this time two of these ruffians had secured me well and while Sandhya tried to reach out for the phone, one of them caught her by the hair, swirled her around and smashed her head onto the floor. He then broke the phone to smithereens and all this while the others kept on searching for something in our rooms.

My daughter, all of two years of age, by then had gone into a state of shock and was numb with fear seeing the violence in her abode. Before one knew, I was bundled off rudely by the intruders and made to descend, kicked and pushed all along, via the stairs onto the lobby.

I noticed by now the night receptionist and our security, both locals, tied firmly to the lobby pillars and securely gagged.

Soon I was blindfolded and strapped onto a Jeep. We were being driven on the smooth state highway, I could feel. The six of them who accompanied me seemed mighty pleased with their catch and were singing along, while taking precautions to ensure that I do nothing stupid as plotting an escape. I was too weak anyway and shocked, wondering how Sandhya and my child were faring by now.

After negotiating the highway and a few bumpy strips on the valley, driven extremely rash by our singer-driver, we reached a gated complex, a farmhouse of sorts, I imagined.

No sooner than entering I was tied firmly to a tree and in that darkness, my blinds taken off. I could see an open fire, few more goons wearing pahari shawls, couple of them playing cards and all of them drinking some hooch.

Taking turns to mete out further torture on me by raining severe punches, slaps and kicks, I was by now seriously injured. Bleeding all over, one eye busted, lips gashed and a possible rib fracture.

In broken Hindi their Sardar now announced, "Wait for Boss and you will see what happens then. Dare you speak a word of this to anyone, we will see to it that your family is finished right in front of your eyes," he hissed!

Soon enough their *Boss* arrived in a limo accompanied by three more of his sidekicks. A comical short statured fella the *Boss*, I mused despite my predicament!

Adorning a bell bottom trouser, long coat, a cowboy hat and a pipe on his lips – without any warning he fished out a revolver from his coat and pressed it on my forehead. "Bagga, you dog, nikal mera tees lakh," he shouted in true filmi style! Out with my thirty lakhs - he demanded.

A flash of lightning struck me as I recalled this fellow now. Mr. Kumar was the Minister for Forestry and a notorious character of sorts by all rights.

"Kumar saab I am not Bagga, you have been misled. I am Anmol, the new GM at the State Hotel. You need to release me sir," I pleaded.

Kumar's face fell and he looked furious. I asked him to check with the Commissioner of Tourism and that is what he did now. After a few calls from his outpost landline, the interim of which seemed an eternity to me, the Commissioner did finally pick up his phone and to my relief cleared my status.

What transpired in the local language was now well comprehended by me without even understanding a word of the dialect. Kumar was agitation personified and wove the revolver on the faces of the goons pointing directly at the Sardar many a time.

In frustration he fired a round in air and landed up menacingly to me. "You, I am sparing you. A word of this and I will personally have you slaughtered," he spat.

Soon I was bundled off, blindfolded once again and by the wee hours of the morning thrown off the running Jeep right in front of our hotel porch.

In severe pain, it took me quite some time to climb up to our room and collect my thoughts. Our staff who had managed to free themselves by now gathered along with Sandhya, our daughter and I. They were extremely relieved to have me safely back, albeit in an extremely sorry, disillusioned and bruised condition.

The real story

Bagga was a Delhi businessman, a so called *successful* Government contractor and a regular at our hotel each month, staying for weeks on end sometimes.

Kumar of course had quite a few businesses apart from logging, highway construction and some more in the state. Bagga used to always stay in his favourite suite right opposite our official accommodation, and it is here that the error of judgement occured. The goons had come to pick up Bagga after he possibly defaulted on a slush payment to the *Boss*!

Instead, they got me…

In fact, Bagga was missing since last evening. The Police, who had by now swooped in, entered the suite opposite mine and found nothing except a few pieces of clothes strewn about and an empty suitcase. Since Bagga often paid for his stay in advance, it dawned upon us that he might have closed his tab, which we found to be true, and had smoothly checked out.

He would have collected his payment for services from the State Exchequer and without handing Kumar's payoff, flown the nest. This is where the confusion ensued and I got dragged in.

Heavens!

What followed next was some ordeal even I did not imagine could occur. While I tried getting myself treated at the State Hospital, I soon realised that Kumar's reputation had the docs shivering there too. Word had reached that I was a victim of his misdeed and though they wanted to assist, they would just not come forward for fear of retribution.

As a result, I was refused treatment.

By evening pretty much under cover, I got medication and treatment via kind mercies of a private practitioner in town.

In the interim, something even stranger started brewing, all by itself.

I had filed my report to our corporate office and the State Tourism Commissioner as I was expected to. News had leaked and before I realised, an anti Kumar lobby of state politicos, students and even our very own hotel workers' trade union called for a general strike.

A rasta-roko also ensued and the entire incident went viral.

In a week, Kumar was forced to release a public apology which he did without divulging his direct involvement though. His statement blamed some of his *disgruntled* party men who in collusion with *certain* opposition members

Carried out this extortion like activity and that an *enquiry commission* would soon go into the depth of this matter to bring the *culprits* to book.

Our corporate office, which had a contract with the State for managing this property, swung into action and the hotel was soon handed back to them to operate, as was earlier.

Sandhya, my daughter and I left the beautiful hills and its lovely surroundings, albeit once again for the plains, having been served an order to manage another property – a beach resort this time!

Just another day in the life of a Hotel GM, I mused…

"Mama always said life is like a box of chocolates. You never know what you're gonna get."

Forrest Gump, 1994

Accounts Receivable

In the mid 80's I was stationed at one of the largest hotels in a Southern metro of India.

We used to be extremely busy year round I remember. Film shoots, weddings, corporate travel, conventions – just name the segment of work and we were one of the top choices.

Coupled with these, our restaurants and bars were iconic in their own right and we had a huge following for our Indian, Chinese, French outlets as well as our All Day Diner which was indeed the talk of the town.

This made my own job as the Food and Beverage head quite a 24x7 affair and since I was housed on the premise, the thin line of work-life balance had long vanished.

Nonetheless, it was a pleasure working for the most sought after hotel in the city and many of us had managed to gather quite a few good friends among our guests who visited us ever so often.

One evening, after our routine friendly table tennis practice among team members, which was a daily stress-buster-do for us, we had gathered at my office. This space incidentally coupled up as the Banquets or events booking venue too.

Most of my colleagues having left for the day, my Banquet Manager and I were chatting up when in walked a gentleman in a flamboyant Pathani Suit, quite uncommon those days in a southern town.

Heavy set he was and carried with him, I still remember, a large tin of Pan Parag sort of a supari mix and a Dunhill cigarette pack in one hand. On his other hand he carried a shining croc leather briefcase.

He sported an open buttoned kurta displaying a heavy gold chain and on one of his hands flashed an equally thick bracelet.

He swaggered in and without wishing us plainly plonked into a sofa. "Give me an ashtray," he demanded.

We wished him jointly and Sarin, our Banquet Manager, obliged him immediately with an ashtray.

"I wish to book the best venue for my son's first birthday."

That was indeed our business so we got down talking. It turned out he wanted a never before hosted lavish sort of an extravaganza for the birthday of his son, and started listing some pretty heavy requests.

Could our staff dress up as dancers in an Arabic palace, could a real dumba be made, and more. Now these were days much before *event organisers* had cropped up and we would be handling all such requests internally.

Dumba in its real sense is a spit fired large piece of meat as whole lamb combined with other delicacies, then further stuffed with forcemeat and dry fruits all of which is slowly open roasted. A treat for the eyes and palate but indeed a specialty to handle.

I was just not sure if Arvind, my Head Chef would be able to manage that.

Anyways, the list continued with demands of two dozen swans (later toned down to large white ducks) to be set afloat on our swimming pool, the entire hotel frontage to be flood lit, every guest in the hotel on that day to be complimented a free glass of bubbly, two camels to be positioned outside the port cochere, half a dozen girls in Arabian Night costumes to sprinkle fragrant rose water on all incoming guests and on and on…

Sarin and I kept nodding and noting till our guest ran out of steam and ideas. We breathed a sigh of relief!

"I am an Adman," he declared.

By this time Sarin and I had deduced that he is rather a *madman*!

"Costs are not an issue and you need to deliver the best. This party will long be talked about in town. This will make you famous," he predicted!

We got down to discussing the menu and other trivia for this *magnum opus* and after discussions on various aspects including return gifts which were to be presented to all attendees, we gave him a quote.

Even without listening fully to our cost breakdown he fished out few bundles of heavy duty notes and practically threw it on the table.

Sarin got down to collecting and counting those while I kept the *adman* company.

"Ten thousand," Sarin said.

"Whatever, keep it. My office will send in the balance tomorrow," said the *adman.*

We got him a receipt and wished him good night while thanking him for the custom. Without speaking another word our *adman* vanished.

What a strange man I pondered. But, in our trade we keep meeting these fascinating characters day in and out for sure and that is what keeps us going. "Must be loaded," Sarin remarked. Of course, I thought.

In the next few days we started receiving daily calls from this gentleman.

Have you guys organised yourself? Have the girls in your team rehearsed their parts for the Arabian Night saga? Has my electrical contractor met up with your people? This practically went on till the day of the birthday bash.

On the day of the function our lawns were decked up grand, a local celebrity DJ was busy dishing out loud Top Twenty Bollywood hits, guests were busy snacking and the multi deck bar propped up for the occasion was packed. Our hostesses were playing their part, dumba was crackling on the spit roast and the general atmosphere was quite electric!

The party continued till well beyond midnight and when the time came for settlement of the damages which had by then blown to some five lakh rupees, a big sum those days by any standard, somehow our *adman* host was missing!

Sarin asked me to hold on to the venue to look after guests and he personally dashed off to the car park area with the security to look for our man who had supposedly driven up in a bright yellow sports Ferrari that night.

Few minutes later he was back and announced that it appears our *adman* feeling unwell sometime in the later part of the evening, had slipped out quietly without *disturbing* his guests.

This he confirmed was the version given by the host when he went to retrieve the keys of his Ferrari from our security post.

His wife who was still at the venue with other guests said that she is aware of this and she was to proceed back soon. She would surely have our settlement done, first thing the very next morning, she promised.

That was the last we heard from them!

Sarin and I practically called the gentleman's office number which he had given to us, a dozen times the next day only to be told that the number belongs to someone else.

Sarin who was a quiet achiever and a solid citizen type of a character, started showing signs of panic. How could we get our money into the books of the hotel is all that we prayed for now.

Exactly a week later we got a call from our General Manager and in his office we found our astute Finance Head holding a copy of a banquet bill.

He was solemnly explaining default of this huge sum subtly hinting that Sarin and I had perfectly goofed up and that we should be held squarely responsible.

Big boss was a no-nonsense man and gave Sarin and I a week's time to sort out this financial mess or else…

By then all of us were fairly well known in the social circles of our town. We were meeting up routinely with the hoi polloi for some business or the other and decided to spread the good word around for letting us know if any of them had an inkling of such a swindler.

To our good luck, a few days later a real gentleman guest of ours' (a tycoon in the *Agarbatti* business, who we had nicknamed *Agarbatti King*) called up.

"Gentlemen, I believe I have your man," he said. That very sentence spurred Sarin and me to leave all that we had to do then and on the excuse of an immediate *sales lead* in town we headed off to meet our lifesaver.

Having got the *adman's* home address from this gentleman and thanking him profusely, we decided to bring this matter to a closure as early as possible.

The very next morning saw the Finance Head, Sarin - our Banquets Head, our Security Chief and I, head off for this defaulter's home located in an upmarket part of the town.

Soon we alighted in front of a bungalow with a perfectly manicured lawn. I walked up through the front gate to the main door. I had no idea whether we would be meeting the defaulter or someone else at this time. I knocked and patiently waited.

The door opened and out stepped a woman in a saree. Mrs. *adman* she was, Sarin and I immediately connected.

"Yes and what may I do for you please?" she asked of us.

Explaining our reason for being there in brief, I asked to be led to Mr. a*dman*.

The lady looked pointedly at me, a bit mysteriously I thought and with a smile on the corner of her lips. She asked us to follow her inside.

All of us followed her inside and while she asked us to be comfortable in her living room, she went off inside her bungalow, leaving us wondering as to what would happen next.

Time went by and soon a maid appeared with a tray of snacks, some sweets and a large pot of hot steaming coffee.

We all were as I remember, pretty taken aback. This was not what we had come in for. All we wanted was a meet up with a defaulter, retrieve our dues and head back. This was a bit too much of warmth, I wondered.

Mrs. *adman* who had by now entered the room, looked up at me directly and said in chaste Bengali which is my native language, "So you have not recognised me yet or have you?"

"Yes I have," I replied. "You are Mr. *adman's* wife and of course it was your child's birthday that we had organised at our hotel."

"Yes that's true," she said, "but you have not recognised me truly." And with this she addressed me by my pet name which none my colleagues knew – at least till then!

"Do you recall your school days at 'St. Thomas' or have you forgotten those too?"

I froze, literally!

It is then that it dawned on me.

My God! I was staring at my close friend from primary school - Anu!

We had not connected for a good decade and half since I moved school to study at Doon.

I felt sorry, both for her and for me. What have I done? All my resentment for this family vanished that very moment and I felt petty for some unexplainable reason.

I should have recognised her earlier and now with my colleagues present I could not even get down to catch up on our childhood memories.

Anu possibly understood my quandary and walked up to me. "Don't worry, I am really sorry for all that happened and even though my husband is not in town, I will make sure I come to your office and pay up," she promised.

What a turn of events and what a day this turned out to be.

Anu did turn up the very next day and settle every cent of the dues.

Despite the payment, for some reason and purely out of emotions I believe, for many months after this incident I blamed myself for having chased a very good friend from school right to her own abode, just to collect money- much like Shylock!

We never met after this and neither did Anu keep in touch.

Life kept me busy with work at the hotel and soon this incident was one of those which fade out in midst of one's demanding schedules.

Were the two happy together, was the *adman* a real cheat or was he going through a genuinely difficult patch, was it guilt of not paying up on time that got Anu to keep aloof? Did I regret chasing an old childhood friend to her very own home purely for money?

Perhaps some questions like these never get a closure.

They choose to remain indistinctly etched in some corner of our hearts and minds *forever*...

"I have always depended on the kindness of strangers."

A Streetcar named Desire, 1951

The Practical Nun

Airports are fun places to work.

In earlier times, when life was considerably innocent and international or domestic gateways as airports were not taken over completely by security personnel, many of the staff working at these venues were issued a *red pass*.

This enabled us to walk up the runway, enter flights and practically go to any space in the airport. Of course, this had to be related to work, but I must admit that was not always the case.

This always brought us in contact with many interesting persons, celebrities, authors, sports persons and so many others going about their lives, flitting across from city to city in that pursuit. One such person who I will always remember is, *Mother*.

In Calcutta (now Kolkata) and possibly all over the country Mother was by far the most revered person for all the work that she was doing against much odds and so very selflessly.

On many occasions we had the opportunity to catch up with her while she would be traveling to various places. I have never seen her using the VIP Lounge at the airport and clad simply in a cotton white and blue bordered saree, ever smiling Mother would just walk up as any other to her flight. What a change we always thought from the others. Politicians, bureaucrats and the so called high and mighty industry barons of every hue, who perhaps thought they owned the airport and somehow the aircrafts too.

During that time, we managed every single refreshment outlet in the domestic and international airport and the large restaurant in the venue too while managing a sizeable flight catering unit at the same base.

We also had a base at the then nearby hotel catering for a few international flights. I headed the multiple operations and we were always extremely busy. Between both the venues we were catering innumerous flights, too many delayed flights, constant catering and allied requirements of airlines all along with the many demands from our trade unions.

As with almost all businesses in the city we too were burdened with the legacy of more than one trade unions and their often fantastic and unreasonable demands. In fact, much that could have been achieved successfully was repeatedly lost because of the time spent in appeasing issues related to workmen's *rights*, real and many imaginary, rather than focusing on growing the business.

One day, in the midst of catering to existing flight catering requirements, and Kolkata was a reasonably busy airport then – we were asked to cater to two more private airlines who were just sanctioned licenses to fly by Civil Aviation.

This meant an exponential jump in revenues for the company and we were indeed happy. In any case, we were well staffed and with a bit of careful planning would be able to pull it off. Except for one snag – the trade unions.

Waiting outside the office of the General Manager, my assistant and me wondered – now what? Would we be able to cater to the new airlines or would our competition land this up in their fold? Will the unions be reasonable with us and allow us to conduct business peacefully or would we sink in to their demands of *overtime* and make the business unprofitable? How would Satish-da, our lion of a General Manager, face up to this?

In a few moments the union members who were with our boss, stormed out and we got the message that the meeting did not go down well.

"I told them to keep out and not put up claims for additional allowances or overtime. Will you be able to pull this off?" He asked of us.

Shetty my fearless assistant and I nodded in the affirmative. The job was routine except for a hot spot – the dish wash section, where cutlery, crockery and galley equipment were washed, sanitised and turned around for return flights in an extremely tight time bound scenario, enabling every flight to be catered punctually.

Here lied the real issue. In case dish wash was deliberately delayed and additional staff and allowances sought to counter that – we had a situation. Unions routinely hit out at this soft spot and got away with claims of mega overtime hours for their members. So much so that the three registered unions worked the shift rosters on their own ensuring that the *booty* got distributed evenly. No management staff intervened, as this was an area that was *hot* and a known trouble spot.

"I believe time has come to stop all this nonsense, but how do we do it?" Satish-da threw the gauntlet at us.

Before I could revert, Shetty our young and warm blooded assistant shot back, "Not an issue sir, we will get it to *zero* overtime hours if you back us up."

Satish-da laughed and laughed loud. "This is Calcutta, Shetty. You mean you will not only cater for additional flights, yet not pay any unreasonable allowances and terminate all this uncalled for overtime hours at your dish-wash? Are you serious? Do you know this practice has been existing for a decade now?" He questioned.

"I believe there is a way sir," Shetty replied.

"Go ahead then and give me a plan of action in a week's time," our GM told us. "Good luck guys and be safe," he advised while escorting us out of his office.

The great thing about our leader was that he was an upright individual, always egging us on to try new things, not be afraid of slip ups at our end pushing us to step out of our comfort zones. In fact, he always set us up for success.

The next day Shetty called me and said, "Sir I have fixed up an appointment at Mother's and would you mind coming in at eleven, we have to meet up with her."

What was Shetty thinking, I thought. He was not one to go for charity. Knowing him well, his one and only line was always that of – charity begins at home.

Soon the thought of meeting Mother however brightened me up and I got going. I found Shetty waiting for me already at her premise.

Mother greeted us and asked, "What can I do for you sons?"

Shetty and I were by now familiar with Mother having seen her many a times at the airport and chatting up pleasantries while she waited for her flight. No more than that though.

Living simply so that others may simply live, was the motto that she embodied and she had never asked us for anything and neither did we offer including any offer to volunteer services at her home for elders, a centre located quite near the airport.

"Mother we need help," Shetty pleaded. "And what would that be?" she asked.

Shetty then went on to explain the predicament that we were going through and how we were losing out daily to an unreasonable tirade of trade union demands and how our quality of delivery suffered along with the general frustration that had seeped in among us supervisor folks at the catering centre.

Mother listened keenly and did not utter a single word. Offering us a glass of water she left the room saying that she will be going to Delhi the next day and would we both like to see her off at the airport?

"Can you help train some of our homeless children?" Mother asked.

Shetty and I had come to the airport to meet up with her.

"That is possible, but we do need to pay them something as a stipend, right Mother?"

"That is your call. You could help them gather experience, say at the mechanised dish wash area," she offered. "Do look after their transportation and I am sure you could offer them a square meal. After all you have a good cafeteria I am told," she said.

"How about the unused food items as packed butter, jam, breads, juices? I am told you destroy them. They are nice edible food items and just because you have off-loaded them from a flight why do you throw them away? Can you please ask the airlines if we take these and feed the poor and hungry at our homes? I am sure they would not mind," she implored.

All these seemed immensely possible and what a solution I thought. Mother is helping us with boys from her *home* to work at the most critical and volatile section of our business which is completely controlled by unions and unarguably the cause of negotiations and bargains with them.

In return the payoff seemed extremely affordable!

"In future, can you help train and certify them in other areas too? May be find them a job?" she asked.

The concept of corporate social responsibility was unknown then and I am not even sure if the acronym CSR existed. Now, after many years, I realise this is exactly what she had gently nudged us to do.

"I have to rush; my flight is announced. Give this note to Satish and tell him I really appreciate his seeking out help and help build lives of youngsters in need."

"Tell him to keep a copy of this on his table. It may help others understand that you people are doing a great job! God bless!" she said, and off she went.

I looked at the note and it went something like this…

Dear Hotel Team – Thank you so very much for helping our young children find a footing in life.

God bless – Mother.

I still have this note somewhere and what a game changer this turned out to be.

Satish-da kept a copy of this note beneath his glass topped table facing the incoming union members so that they could clearly read this message from Mother.

The boys from Mother's Home landed up in good numbers and took over the complete dish wash routine, overtime got to zero hours, off-loaded good quality un-tampered food items started getting dispatched to Mother's homes, our own staff were redeployed to areas where they had to put in a honest day's work and the unions kept completely away from the flight kitchen.

Mother was not to be challenged in Calcutta.

She was Calcutta personified, the Practical Nun in the City of Joy!

"Elementary, my dear Watson."

The Adventures of Sherlock Holmes, 1929

Cyber Crime

"Let me take you, Head Constable sir, to my office and show you exactly how this crime happened. It is quite technical you see!"

Our enthusiastic and ever confident Principal, Dr. Prasad was leading the way to his office and the accompanying heavy set police constable looking very officious and a tad puzzled too, followed him matching his footsteps.

Set in a *B town* our college prided itself as a fine hospitality school in the country and though remote in location, drew students from all over the nation including major metros.

We were just four years into operation and were fast gaining a reputation for placement of students at the finest chain of hotels nationally and internationally.

We had a small set of some two hundred students in college and they were all boarders of our hostels situated just beside the institute – girls' hostels being a bit further off.

Our faculty matching the age of the institute were mostly young and a few were recent alumni of the same alma mater. Some of them had chosen to take up teaching as a vocation rather than entering the trade. They were good students who demonstrated a flair for teaching and were handpicked by Dr. Prasad who was himself was a vastly reputed industry trainer of prodigious standing.

Manoj, one of the young teachers who was responsible for teaching Front Desk Operations to the first and second year management students, was already receiving rave praises from his students for his avant-garde methods of instructing. Firmly in his belief that nine tenths of education was all about encouragement, his students related to him and his brand of delivery well. He was current and structured, and he managed to deliver the theory and practical aspects of his curriculum always on time.

He would engage his *team* (read students) often in projects as visiting various city properties, interact with Front Desk Managers of various brands, get over Hotel Managers to the classroom for valuable industry academia parlays, thus setting a very high benchmark of learning and development for young minds.

His students loved him, I would say almost worshipped him. So popular was he.

A month earlier Manoj was to deliver a session on *Handling of Credit Cards*. Two decades ago credit card machines were slowly being converted from manual to automated swipe types, manual charge slips were being replaced and hot list bulletins were something that the new generation students and professionals would never even knew existed.

Technology was setting in and many of us were applying for and getting to taste the power of plastic money for the very first time in our lives. Some still doubted their ability to manage this new change and stayed away. But most of us including Manoj were already in possession of at least one plastic card and were we proud of flashing it across at establishments for our purchases. A new high this was!

Manoj had just applied for and received an Amex Card. Like so many of us he too was so very proud.

Armed with his new gleaming card, Manoj entered his second year Front Office class and started presenting how to handle credit cards at Front Desks of hotels. As always, he had prepared well for his session. His credit card, both back and front with all details including the CVV number, flashed across the classroom screen. Manoj started explaining to his students about merchant banks, digits on credit cards and their significance, date of expiry issues, fundamentals of credit card security et al.

Soon he started getting questions and was happily answering them including when a few queried him on the significance of the CVV number. Charged up to explain to the youngsters, Manoj eagerly told them how this very important three digit number was the key to security when conducting procurements online.

Readers, one must note that online purchases was really in its infancy then and sites as Amazon, Lazada, Best Buy, Flipkart, Snapdeal and Pepperfry and others were not even born. However, there were many other sites and this is where our story takes an interesting turn.

Some bright person in the class at this juncture managed to copy the sixteen digit card number, the date of expiry and CVV number as Manoj not satisfied by only showing details on the screen, was actively passing around this magical plastic money piece to the *team members* to have a look, see and feel, first hand.

Sometime the following month, on one evening, we teachers were gathered around the cafeteria during our free time and generally catching up on small talk and college gossip, when in walked a heavily disturbed Manoj.

"Guys this is not acceptable. How could this happen to me?" Visibly shaken and with a sullen face he sat down and told us his plight. He had just received his monthly credit card bill and was stunned to note that a thousand rupees and more got charged for using services of an *adult site*.

"I have not and never will do this," he wailed! "How did this happen to me? I called up the back office support and they clearly told me that my card has been used. Guys, I have been compromised. My reputation is at stake and to top it all I have to shell out this huge sum."

Many of us sympathised and I remember one amongst us suggested we do a police complaint to catch the culprit. How would that help, I wondered?

Another suggested we must bring it to the attention of our Principal and he in his wise judgement will definitely set this right.

So on to Dr. Prasad's office we marched. Our Principal was a huge bundle of energy and he had a big clout in town. From the District Magistrate to the Police Commissioner to petty bureaucrats he knew them all in person. He was a great outgoing personality, not an academic holed up in his chamber as one normally encountered in many institutions.

"I will call up Sinha right now," he boomed. Meaning the Police Commissioner of the town that is.

"Manoj, do you have any doubts on anyone as of now?"

"No sir," Manoj confided. "I did however show the card and give details to my team."

"Your team?" Dr. Prasad quizzed.

"My fourth sem students sir, while discussing credit card transactions and handling processes as a part of their curriculum."

"I see," Dr. Prasad sighed! "All right the presence of police on campus will surely defuse the culprits and I am sure we will be able to pin the joker down soon," he said.

Before we realised the full potential forte of our Principal's networking skills, the Head Constable of the local police station and one of his junior appeared at the college gates, precisely in ten minutes.

Head Constable Prahlad – a very heavy set guy, wearing a perma frown, charged in and demanded to see our Principal. Manoj gingerly pointed out to our boss.

At this stage Manoj tried to convey that he was the person who was really the affected party but Prahlad was in no mood to listen to some lower rung in the food chain.

Prahlad turned to Manoj and short of shutting him up said, "Aap ko poocha hai kya? Kaun ho tum?" Translated, did I ask you? Who are you? A typical reaction from someone in authority to prove his superiority I thought.

We quickly backed off and Dr. Prasad now took over completely. "Yes Prahladji, let me explain, this is how it all happened," he said and sprinted forward leading the team to his own office.

All of us followed the entourage.

"Hmm… So this is how it happened. Okay, let me know when did it happen?" Demanded Head Constable.

"Err… easy to say as the bill just came in this morning. The date of the transaction is in the bill."

"Bill for what? I thought someone used a computer without permission," came the reply.

"No sir… actually…"

"Actually what Principal Sahib?"

"Sir, actually this is a credit card fraudulent usage situation."

"How can that be? Card is with Manoj you said," retorted Prahlad.

"No sir, actually card is with him but the purchase was made by someone else."

"How can that be? Did he lose his card? Has he made a police report? Where is the FIR? C'mon c'mon show me now."

"No sir, not that way. This was an online purchase."

"Oh that way, so what is the problem?"

"Sir, the purchase was not done by Manoj." "If not then by who?"

"That's what we don't know."

"Ok then explain Dr. saab how can one purchase over the internet when the card is with someone else?" queried Prahlad.

"Ah… that is easy sir. Let me show you." With this Dr. Prasad logged on a retail site on the internet and went on to explain enthusiastically how a magazine could be procured by just knowing the card number, expiry date and CVV number, no matter where the card was and with who. Internet security passwords and OTP numbers were not really required those days as the CVV number was solely sacrosanct then, if you recall.

I am not sure how much of this got registered in the Head Constable's mind but his junior sure nodded his head vigorously as if he understood the whole lesson fully well.

This did not go down too well with the boss who shot an icy question immediately to his junior, "Tere ko samajh ayee kya? You got it I hope? Then write a report for me to take back in five minutes, okay?"

That suitably dampened his junior's mood and we were quite sure that the duo has still not completely got the situation wrapped up.

Prahlad soon bowled a *googly*.

"Very well Principal Sahib, since this is the scene of the crime and now that you have explained it so well, we must confiscate your computer."

"Why, why sir?" Clearly puzzled, Dr. Prasad pleaded.

"Why, it is you who just showed us how the crime has occurred and surely it must the equipment that carried it out. This equipment is vital for us to present in court as *evidence* and that is why we must confiscate this, sir. Can you also come to the Thana with us now and record all that you explained?"

This put all of us in a major quandary and we wondered whether we are getting any help from authorities or is this whole episode dragging us deeper into trouble?

Fortunately, Dr. Prasad went into another round of a theory session with the police immediately and pounced on them with a ten minute presentation on how the internet world is virtual and that such illegal procurement could have been carried out from any terminal from any other office of the institute as well. Clearly that should save the day we all thought.

"Theek hai then, we would like all the computers to be handed over to us for the investigation, now that you have so clearly explained the situation," directed the constable.

By now we did not know whether to cry, laugh or tear our hair except acknowledge the fact that we were getting into some deep mess all right. At this stage, some of us tried to explain the finer points of internet based purchase and that it could have been done by anyone, even from across the road Net Cafe, right opposite the gate of the college.

"That being the case we must confiscate their machines too," summarised our excited Head Constable!

Finally, after a few rounds of such hilarious repeated questioning and our persuasive attempts to make the powers that be understand the mechanics of the newly evolved aspects of the world-wide web, the constable apparently understood that we as teachers nor Dr. Prasad had any direct role in this *crime*. We were ostensibly duped by someone and that we needed their support in solving this matter.

"Fair enough," chirped the head man. "Manoj come over to the station and log in a report. We will get into the depth of this matter."

Soon Manoj vanished to the local station with the duo, thankfully without our Principal's Desktop in tow, and logged in a report as advised.

Cyber Crime | 113

The next morning as I reported for my work, I found groups of students gathered around the college cafeteria and in hushed voices discussing something grave.

Now what? I thought.

A second-year management student came forward and handed me the local English Daily.

"Is this true sir?" She asked.

First Cyber Crime in Town, the headline shrieked.

Oh God! We are now famous, I immediately thought, of course with all the wrong connotations.

A photo of the Head Constable, Manoj, the constable's assistant and his seniors, all of them beaming except Manoj, who was staring sheepishly to the ground as if he was the guilty party, followed the headline.

A good three para article detailed the proficiency with which a cyber - crime, previously unheard of, was unearthed by the local police team under the able direction of the seniors in constabulary at a prestigious institution of the town and that a 'foreign hand' cannot be ruled out at all, it reported.

'Investigations are on the way' it read, paying rich tributes to the manner in which the *crime* was unearthed and how efficiently and promptly was the matter brought to books.

Nowhere did it mention as to who the culprit was or how did the whole episode take shape.

As it happens in close knit places, especially institutions where information flow is tapped for *discipline* and keeping matters under tab, by the weekend we got our scoop from some rival students (read college spies) on who had exactly carried this out.

The *criminal* as it happened just could not hide his glee in committing this delinquency and was heard bragging after a few rounds of beer, in a popular nearby watering hole aptly nick-named *The Thirsty Scholar*. He would soon negotiate another conquest - he was heard announcing, meaning carry out another fresh on - line transaction.

Thank goodness Manoj had decided by then to join the conservative *no credit card* gang having cut up his plastic pleasure and thrown it away for good.

Master criminal was quickly apprehended by us and punished internally by means of extra projects, hard time lines for academic submissions and helping our librarian sort out the college library on three consecutive Sundays.

Soon the *master criminal* joined our elite band of college spies and as I recall, helped us unearth quite a few difficult mysteries till he passed out of his undergrad course.

Neither the constabulary nor Dr. Pandey were given any further lead into the first ever cyber - crime of our town.

Last heard, *master criminal* was doing pretty well in life working as Vice President with a leading merchant banker in the United States.

God bless him…

About the Author

Across the globe Sandip Mukherjee has successfully headed hotels, resorts, state houses, international chain of restaurants and hospitality institutes for four decades and more.

He has been the Director of Operations for Luxury Hotels, Palaces and Resorts for the Taj Group of Hotels.

Sandip is now a Hospitality trainer, consultant and academic based out of Kolkata. He often works pro bono cutting across a spectrum of businesses. He has a rich and successful track of people driven leadership. This is his first published venture.

He can be reached at: copavillaglobal@gmail.com

CPSIA information can be obtained
at www.ICGtesting.com
Printed in the USA
LVHW010451231121
704213LV00004B/311